RUPERT™
and the Sorcerer's Apprentice

by Ian Robinson
Illustrated by Marjorie Owens

Methuen Children's Books

One day Rupert and his chums were playing football on Nutwood Common when they heard a humming sound. Looking up, they were amazed to see a strange object streaking across the sky towards them.

"It's a flying saucer!" cried Bill.

"You're right!" gasped Rupert. "It's coming this way."

As the pals stared in astonishment, the saucer swooped over their heads and landed on top of a nearby hill.

"Come on!" cried Podgy. "Let's go and see what it is!"

He raced up the hill towards it with the others following close behind him.

It turned out to be a hollow dish with a seat in the middle.

On the seat was a young boy dressed in brightly-coloured
clothes. He waved as he saw the chums.

    "Hello," stammered Rupert. "W. . . welcome to Nutwood."

    "Greetings!" said the boy, stepping out of the flying
saucer. "My name is Ziz. I have travelled far to reach your
village and have much to do before I can return."

Ziz explained that he was the apprentice of a powerful magician. "Unfortunately, my master was halfway through a complicated spell when he ran out of magic powder. He sent me to see if I can get some more from his friend, the Chinese Conjurer. Do you know him?"

"Yes, I do," said Rupert.

Rupert offered to take Ziz to the Conjurer's house. The pair set off and, before long, they saw a tall tower among the trees.

"That's the Conjurer's pagoda," said Rupert. "He lives there with his daughter, Tigerlily."

At the pagoda Rupert knocked on the door.

A moment later the Conjurer appeared at the door and
Rupert explained to him that Ziz had come to Nutwood on a
special mission.

"I remember your master well," said the Conjurer to the
young boy. "It will be an honour to be of service. Come
inside and tell me what it is you seek."

The Conjurer listened to the apprentice's tale. "I am sure I can help your master," he smiled.

He took down a large book and started to leaf through the pages. He soon found the spell he needed, but said the magic powder would take a long time to prepare.

"You must stay with us until it is ready," he told Ziz.

While the Conjurer got down to work, Tigerlily and Rupert
decided to show Ziz around Nutwood. On the way, Ziz told
Rupert how grateful he was for his help.

"I would like to thank you by granting you a wish!" he said.

"Can you really grant wishes?" asked Tigerlily.

"Of course!" said the boy. "I, too, am a magician."

"What would you like, Rupert?" asked the boy.

"How about a sponge cake I can take to my parents for their afternoon tea?" said Rupert.

"That's easy!" laughed Ziz, and he chanted a special rhyme. All at once, the air was full of stars, and Rupert was engulfed in a cloud of coloured smoke.

As the smoke cleared, Tigerlily started to giggle. Instead of the sponge cake he had asked for, Rupert was holding an enormous bathroom sponge!

"Oh dear!" sighed Ziz. "All my spells seem to go wrong like this!"

"Making magic isn't easy," agreed Tigerlily.

"Why don't you try again?" suggested Tigerlily.

"All right," said Ziz. "But this time it is your turn to ask for something, Tigerlily."

Tigerlily thought hard. "What I'd really like is for winter to be over and spring to begin," she declared. "Now let's see if you can do that!"

"That is a difficult spell," said Ziz. "I will try my best and see what happens."

As Rupert and Tigerlily looked on, he shut his eyes and started to chant a spell. "Abracadabra! Let spring start. It's time for winter to depart!"

Once again, the air was filled with smoke and stars.

This time, when the mist cleared, Rupert and Tigerlily gasped in astonishment. Daffodils and tulips had sprung up, all in full bloom, and the branches of the trees were covered in pink blossom. Rupert could scarcely believe his eyes. Spring really had come to Nutwood.

"It worked!" cried Ziz. "I did it!"

That afternoon, when Rupert went home for tea, he told his parents about Ziz and how he made spring start early by working a magic spell.

"It *is* milder all of a sudden," agreed Mrs Bear.

"My barometer says fair," added Mr Bear. "It looks as if your friend's good weather might last."

As Rupert drifted off to sleep that night, he suddenly heard a gentle tapping at the window. Drawing back the curtain, he spotted a little man, whom he recognised as one of Nutwood's Imps of Spring.

"I'm sorry to wake you," the Imp said as he climbed into the room.

"Something very strange has happened to the seasons," said
the Imp. "Spring isn't due to start for ages yet, but all of a
sudden the trees in Nutwood have started to blossom and all
the flowers are in bloom. One of our Imps thinks it's because
of the strange boy we saw you with this afternoon. Is he
some sort of magician?"

Although he didn't want to get Ziz into trouble, Rupert had
to admit that the Sorcerer's apprentice was to blame for the
sudden change in Nutwood's season.

"I'm sure he didn't realise he was doing anything wrong,"
he told the Imp. "I'll talk to him in the morning and ask him
to undo the spell."

Next day, Rupert set out for Tigerlily's house as soon as he had finished breakfast.

"I'm afraid Ziz and Tigerlily have already left," the Conjurer told him when he arrived. "They went into Nutwood earlier this morning, so that Ziz could see the sights while I finish the powder his master needs."

Rupert hurried into Nutwood to see if he could find the pair.
He walked anxiously down the High Street looking for them,
and was relieved to meet Tigerlily coming the other way.

"Thank goodness you are here!" she cried, catching sight
of him. "I was about to come and ask you for help."

"Why?" gasped Rupert. "What's wrong?"

Tigerlily explained that Ziz had been causing chaos in Nutwood by granting all the wishes he overheard as he walked along the High Street.

"What's wrong with that?" asked Rupert.

"People don't always get exactly what they wished for," said Tigerlily. "Come and see."

As the pair set off down the road, they met Podgy, carrying a fully-laden breakfast tray.

"I was so hungry, I wished I could have breakfast all over again," he admitted sheepishly.

Before the pals could explain about Ziz, they heard a commotion at the end of the street.

"It's Constable Growler!" cried Rupert. "But what's he doing wearing pyjamas?"

"I was so sleepy, I wished I was back in bed," explained the embarrassed policeman.

"We've got to find Ziz!" declared Tigerlily. "Who knows what he'll do next?"

"There he is!" cried Rupert, and they ran towards him.

"Hello!" called Ziz. "Isn't this marvellous? I had no idea that granting wishes would be such fun!"

"This can't go on," Rupert told him. "You've got to stop!"

"Why?" asked the boy. "The more I practise, the better my spells will be."

"That's just the problem," said Rupert. "Your spell to make all the trees blossom worked so well it upset the Imps of Spring. They're worried that all the flowers will be used up too early so there'll be none left when spring really should begin. They want you to put the seasons back to normal again. Please, Ziz, you have to undo your spells."

Ziz looked downcast at Rupert's request, and then shook
his head.

"You don't understand!" he said. "I can't undo the spells.
I haven't been taught how."

Tigerlily thought hard for a few moments, then told Ziz
he'd have to ask her father to help bring back winter.

"Oh dear," the apprentice sighed. "If he tells my master what has happened, I will get into trouble for making magic without permission."

"Don't worry," said Tigerlily, "I'm sure my father will understand that you didn't mean any harm."

"That's right," said Rupert. "Let's go and see him."

Tigerlily's father chuckled when they told him about Podgy's breakfast and P.C. Growler in his pyjamas, but when he heard how Ziz had upset the Imps of Spring, he agreed to put things right straight away.

"It's lucky magic works backwards," he said and started to chant a powerful spell.

A flash of bright light filled the air and the blossom on the trees disappeared as suddenly as it had arrived.

Ziz smiled with relief. "I am so glad everything is all right again," he said.

"Let's go back to the pagoda," the Conjurer told him. "The powder that your master needs is now ready."

"Learn a lesson from your visit to Nutwood," said the
Conjurer as he handed Ziz the flask of powder. "There's
more to magic than learning spells. Remember that and
you'll become a magician your master can be proud of."

"Will you tell him . . . ?" began Ziz.

"I will simply say he has a promising apprentice!" smiled the Conjurer. "Now hurry back and see he gets this safely."

"Goodbye!" called Rupert and Tigerlily as they watched Ziz take off in his flying saucer.

"Farewell," he cried. "And thank you for all your help!"

Adapted from *Rupert and the Sorcerer's Apprentice*
by Ian Robinson
First published in Great Britain in 1992 in *The Sunday Express Magazine*
Copyright © 1992 Express Newspapers plc

This edition first published in Great Britain in 1993
by Methuen Children's Books
an imprint of Reed Consumer Books Limited
Michelin House, 81 Fulham Road, London SW3 6RB
and Auckland, Melbourne, Singapore and Toronto

ISBN 0 416 18831 1

Printed in Great Britain